Little Else

ON THE RUN

To Gracie and Sol
J.H

To Quinn and Theo
B.N

Little Else

ON THE RUN

Julie Hunt & Beth Norling

ALLEN&UNWIN

The Wild Roaming Life

When **Little Else** left her grandmother's hut
she took nothing except a bag of apples,
a blanket and a lucky horseshoe nail that used to
belong to her grandfather. She was wearing the
cowgirl costume from her trick-riding act at the
circus and she was riding Outlaw, a horse who
used to belong to a bushranger. She headed west
on the road to Mt Direction. Outlaw galloped
to the top of Split Rock Hill then settled into
a steady trot. Little Else leaned along his neck.

'Tell me about the Wild Roaming Life,'
she whispered.

The big horse tossed his head. 'A bushranger's
life is never dull,' he snorted. 'You move like
lightning and you never strike the same
place twice.'

'Talking to yourself again, Little Else?' It was the postman, riding along with his mailbag.

'No. I'm talking to Outlaw.'

The postman laughed.

'Where are you heading?' he asked.

'We're off to find the Wild Roaming Life.' Little Else looked over the postman's shoulder towards the hills. The postman raised his eyebrows.

'Does your grandmother know?'

'Of course!' said Little Else, and she did a quick handstand on the saddle. 'She knows I can't keep still for long.'

'Good luck to you then. Don't forget to write home.' The postman raised his hat and continued on his way.

'Go on, Outlaw,' said Little Else. 'Tell me more.'

'The rugged hills give you cover and the mountains are your friends. You sleep with one eye open and you're always on the run.'

'But we're not on the run,' said Little Else.

'That's because we haven't done anything yet.'

There was noise up ahead: cowbells and
bellowing and someone shouting. Little Else
came over the brow of the hill and saw a
team of bullocks trying to haul a heavy wagon.
One wheel was stuck in a rut. The animals
were hot and tired.

'Pull, you lazy beasts!' yelled the bullock driver.
'You up front – Bonehead! Wake up!' He flicked
his whip above the horns of the lead bullock.

'Stop that!' said Little Else.

The man looked up. 'Nice horse,' he said. 'Wide shoulders. Powerful chest.'

'He used to belong to Harry Blast,' Little Else told him.

'The bushranger?' said the man. 'Heard of him. And I've heard of his horse. They say he's a rogue.'

'How can he be a rogue if I'm riding him?'

'True enough.' The bullock driver wiped his brow.

'He's quiet and well behaved,' said Little Else. 'Do you want to try him?'

'Can't hurt,' said the man. 'It'll be something to tell them when I get this load to town. I've ridden a bushranger's horse.'

Little Else slipped off and the bullock driver got on. Immediately Outlaw shot off down the track at full gallop.

'Whoa!' yelled the man. 'Steady up.'

Little Else waited until she could no longer hear his cries, then she quietly unyoked the bullock team.

'No one deserves to be called Bonehead,'
she said to the leader.
'I will call you Edward Longhorn.'

The bullock lowered his head and walked
off into the bush, taking the team with him.
Little Else heard the clanking of his bell
getting fainter and fainter.

When Outlaw arrived back he wasn't even
blowing. There was no sign of the bullock driver.
Little Else hopped on.

'That's one good deed for the day,' she said.

'Bushrangers don't do good deeds,'
Outlaw snorted.

'This one does,' said Little Else.

Reward

Little Else picked a mountain in the distance and headed towards it.

'That's Mt Long Gone,' Outlaw told her. 'It's five days ride from Three-Cow Flat.'

Every evening she lit a fire and sang songs about the wild country they were passing through. She slept peacefully under the stars. Each morning she woke up with the sun in her eyes and a smile on her face.

'This is the life,' she said. 'When we reach a town, I'll send a postcard to Grandma and tell her that I love this life even more than the circus.'

When she reached a turn-off that said Ploughman's Bend, she took it.

'We'll get supplies there, then travel on towards Three-Cow Flat.'

They had not gone far along the Ploughman's Bend road when Little Else noticed a sign nailed on a tree. There was a picture of a girl that looked a bit like her. WANTED, it said. FOR CATTLE DUFFING.

Little Else peered at the sign. 'It *is* me!' she cried. Her mouth fell open as she read the notice.

WANTED

FOR CATTLE DUFFING.
Little Else, formerly La Petite Elsié,
Expert Trick Rider and Horse Whisperer,
now turned Cattle Thief.
Stole a Team of Bullocks
on April 1st near Split Rock.

REWARD

There was a description under the picture.

LITTLE ELSE

7 years of Age, stands as high as a Small Pony.
Strong and Supple build. Eyes – Hazel.
Wearing Cowgirl Outfit with Fringe and Tassel.
Hair unkempt & of Wild Appearance.
Shirt – Blue Flannel embroidered with Swirls.

'That's not true,' said Little Else.
'They're stars not swirls!'

At the bottom of the sign was
the word REWARD in big letters.

'Perhaps I should give myself up,'
she said. 'I could explain the situation
and collect the reward.'

'It doesn't work like that.' Outlaw looked
over his shoulder. 'From now on we'll
travel by night and rest in the daytime.'

'But then we'll miss out on
seeing the countryside.'

'It can't be helped,' said Outlaw.
'We have to sleep with one eye open.'

Postcards

L ittle Else wrote postcards to her Grandma but she didn't post them. She kept them in her saddlebag.

Dear Gran,

Lucky Outlaw is sure-footed. We travel in the dark and try and keep off the main roads. When we stop I practise my flips and tumbles. Outlaw says I should keep still because we're on the run and have to be careful. I don't really feel like a bushranger. If I was going to be a proper bushranger I would need a gang.

Your loving grand-daughter,

Little Else
xX

Dear Gran,

I am sitting high up under a rocky ledge. You should see the view! Outlaw is grazing a short distance away. I have finished the apples and now I'm eating berries. Today I made up a lovely song about cliffs and boulders. I will sing all my songs to you when I come back to Stony Gully.

Your loving grand-daughter,

Little Else XxX

PS Don't forget to prune the apple tree this winter. Are the hens still laying?

Dear Gran,

Sometimes we hear voices in the distance and the clinking of chains. Outlaw says prisoners are building the roads and I have to be careful not to be caught. I would like to go to a town and find a post office so I can post my cards to you. But we have to stay out of sight.

How is 24 Carrot? Tell her she will always be my favourite donkey.

Your loving grand-daughter,

Little Else xXxXx

PS Have you dug the potatoes yet?

The knackers

Little Else was skirting the town of Three-Cow Flat when she came across a strange sort of farm. She saw stockyards and bare paddocks and barbed-wire fences. Horses stood around an old tin shed. Their heads were down and their ears were back.

'What is this place?' she asked.

Outlaw shuddered. 'It's the knackers,' he said. 'The end of the road.'

A grey mare with one blind eye came up to the fence. She was silver in the moonlight.

'I used to be a champion racehorse,' she whispered. 'Now I'm a broken-down nag, only good for dog meat.'

'Don't say that!' Little Else slipped to the ground.

'I can see you are travellers,' the mare said. 'Have you ever heard of a place called Mt Lost?'

'Yes,' said Outlaw. 'It's somewhere east of the Lower Hope Ranges.'

'They say there is a place beyond that mountain where the pasture is knee deep and apple trees grow wild. They say if you go there you will never be found.'

'I don't know about that,' said Little Else. 'But it sounds better than here. I'm opening the gates.'

Little Else slipped through the fence. She ran towards the yards and opened every gate she could see. The horses filed past. Little Else saw sway backs and splayed hoofs. There were ponies with knobbly knees and broken-winded hacks who could barely raise a trot. Soon there were only two horses left, the grey mare and an ancient cart horse with a shaggy coat and great feathered hoofs.

'Leave me,' he said. 'I'm past it. I'm over the hill.'

'No. I'm not leaving anyone,' said Little Else.

The old cart horse plodded solemnly through the gate. 'Much obliged,' he said as he made his way to freedom.

The old Knackery

The grey mare was the last horse to leave.

'If you don't make it to that land where the apple trees grow, you can always go to my grandma's place in Stony Gully. She'll look after you. It's past Split Rock on the way to...'

Just then a dog barked and a light came on in the shed.

'Look out!' said Outlaw.

Little Else ran to the fence. As she was getting through, one of her tassels got caught on the wire. A door banged.

'Hold it!' someone shouted.

Little Else ripped the tassel off and leapt into the saddle. The knacker's horses went one way and Outlaw went the other.

'Let's hope they make it,' Little Else whispered as she galloped into the night.

The gang

'**O**utlaw, wake up!'
Outlaw snorted and sat up in
the clearing where they had slept.

'I was dreaming of that place the
grey mare talked about,' he said.

'Shhh. Listen!'

There was a clanking of chains and the sound
of picks and shovels. Outlaw's ears flickered.
He stood up. Little Else peered through the trees.

'Work faster, you lazy scoundrels.'

A guard was walking up and down cracking
his whip. Men were breaking stone.

'That's so unfair,' whispered Little Else.

'Come away,' Outlaw said. 'We shouldn't have
stopped here. We're too close to the road.'

Little Else didn't move.

'Bend your backs! I want this road finished by the end of the month,' the guard shouted. 'Get stuck into it.'

How rude, Little Else thought.

Outlaw was restless. 'Come away. There's nothing you can do.'

Little Else put her hands on her hips. 'Yes, there is,' she said. She stepped out into the open. Outlaw stayed hidden. 'Why are these men in chains?' Little Else asked the guard.

'Because they're a chain gang,' the man replied. 'Dangerous criminals.'

Little Else looked at the prisoners. They didn't look dangerous. They looked worn out. The guard's horse was tied to a tree. Her head was down and her ribs were sticking out. She had the same look as the prisoners.

'Your horse is too thin.'

'Out of my way, girl,' said the guard. 'I've got work to do.'

'No, really,' said Little Else. 'You need a better horse than that.'

'No doubt,' said the guard. 'But a good horse is hard to find.

They don't give guards like me good horses. Even the police don't have good horses.'

'I've got a good horse.' Little Else whistled and Outlaw stepped reluctantly forward.

'I never had this trouble with Harry Blast,' he muttered under his breath.

The chain gang stared. The guard's horse looked up.

'How did you come by a horse like that?'

'It's a long story,' said Little Else. 'You wouldn't have time to listen. You've got a road to build.'

'That's right,' said the guard.

'Tell you what,' said Little Else. 'Let's do a swap. This horse is too big and strong for a small girl like me. How about I take your horse and you take mine?

The guard's mouth fell open. He couldn't believe his luck. 'You're on,' he said.

'You'll have to try him out of course,' said Little Else.

The guard put down his whip and walked over to Outlaw.

'He can be a handful at times,' said Little Else.

'Managing horses is the same as managing

a chain gang. You show them who's boss
and you never have any trouble.'

The guard sprang into the saddle.

'Whoa up. Steady, you wild mongrel.
Halt!' he yelled as Outlaw bolted into the bush.

The chain gang put down their tools. They
looked at the spot where the guard disappeared
into the scrub, then they looked at Little Else.

'You've lost your horse,' said the guard's mare.

'He'll come back.'

'She's talking to herself,' one of the prisoners said.

'No, I'm talking to the horse. My name is Little Else, trick rider and horse whisperer.'

'Jack Stubbs,' said the prisoner. 'Bootmaker and petty thief.'

'Dan Bakehouse,' said the man next to him. 'Breadmaker and desperado.'

'Firebolt Jim,' said the next man in line. He had a thick beard and a hole in his cheek.

'I know your horse. I helped Harry Blast blow up the Boomtown Bank.'

'You did?' Little Else's eyes grew wide.
'Are you a bushranger?'

'Used to be,' said Firebolt. 'Until I got caught.'

'Would you like to be one again?'

'Certainly would,' said Firebolt Jim.

Just then, Outlaw came crashing back through the bush. The guard was gone. 'Must have dropped him off under a low bough,' said Firebolt Jim. 'Do you think he could carry all of us?'

'Of course,' said Little Else.

'What, four grown men in chains?'

'He can do it,' said Little Else. 'Up you get.'

She helped them onto Outlaw's enormous back.

'We'll need a blacksmith,' she said. 'To get rid of your leg-irons.'

'There's one in Witt's End,' they told her.

They set off at a steady pace. Little Else
sat in front. Jack Stubbs sat behind her.

'I've heard of you,' he said.
'You're a cattle duffer and horse rustler.'

'And now I'm the leader of a gang
of bushrangers.'

'Whacko,' said Jack Stubbs. 'I think
I'll change my name to Lightning Jack!'

'And I'll be Dangerous Dan,'
said Dan Bakehouse.

There was a man sitting behind
Firebolt Jim. He had a lean and hungry look.

'What's your name?' Little Else asked.

'That's Hollow-Gut Reed,' said Dan.

They continued on in silence and reached
the edge of Witt's End just as it was getting dark.

'Wait here,' said Little Else. 'I'll go and find the
blacksmith's shop.'

'Be quick,' Outlaw whispered.

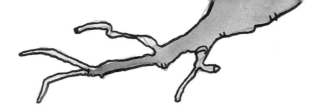

Stony Gully

'Nothing again?' Little Else's grandmother asked the postman.

The postman shook his head.

'I'm sure she'll write when she has time,' Grandma said.

'Look at these.' The postman took a handful of newspapers from his saddlebag. Little Else's grandmother read the headlines.

LITTLE ELSE WANTED FOR CATTLE DUFFING

Little Else steals horses near Witt's End – tassel found on barbed-wire fence

'You should have kept a tighter rein on her,' said the postman.

'Well it's no good shutting the stable door after the horse has bolted,' said Grandma.

She took the newspapers inside her hut and stuck them up on the wall next to the articles about Little Else's career in the circus. Then she sat down to write Little Else a letter.

Dear Little Else,

I'm sure you have a good reason for everything you do. I miss you and look forward to the day when you come home to Stony Gully, but make sure you have enough adventures first.

24 Carrot is well and I have dug the potatoes and put in the broad beans. There is a postcard here for you from Harry Blast and your friends from the circus. There's a lovely picture of you on the front doing that triple-backflip at full gallop.

All my love,
Grandma x X x X x X x X x X x X x

She read the letter aloud then put it in an
envelope and addressed it to:

Little Else,
Notorious Bushranger,
c/o PO Witt's End

She doubted that Little Else would be checking
her mail but it felt good to write.

Iron Bob

The blacksmith's name was Iron Bob. He was covered in soot and sweat and he wore a leather apron.

'Hail!' he shouted when he noticed Little Else in the doorway. 'What a marvellous thing it is to be a blacksmith!' His hammer rang down on the anvil and he shouted over the noise. 'Iron from the earth, air through the bellows, fire in the forge and water... Do you know about the water?'

'Look, I'm in a hurry,' said Little Else.

Iron Bob didn't hear her. He took a piece of red-hot iron and plunged it into a water trough. It made a mighty hiss. For a moment he disappeared in steam.

'Water for the magic power of strength!

Do you know how much stronger this metal is
now it's been cooled in the water?'

Little Else shook her head.

'One hundred and fifty times!'
the blacksmith cried. 'Isn't that astounding?'

'Yes it is,' shouted Little Else.

'What can I do for you?' Iron Bob put
down his tools. Little Else was
about to speak when he
raised his hand.

'I know,' he said. 'You want to learn the trade.
'You want to be a magician with metal like me.
You're small but I can see you're strong. I need
an apprentice. The answer is yes!'

'But I don't want to be a blacksmith…'

Iron Bob held up his hand. There was the
sound of horses outside. He put his finger to
his lips then he upended a drum and put it
down over Little Else. Suddenly
she was in darkness.
Iron Bob started
hammering again.

'A blacksmith is as strong
as an ox. Burnt black by the
blast of the furnace, sooty
with coal smoke. All day long
he wrestles the hard metal…'

'Good evening, Iron Bob,'
a voice interrupted. It was the
guard from the chain gang.
Little Else crouched down in the drum.

'We're looking for four men in leg-irons,'
came a second voice. 'Rogues and villains,
every one of them.'

Iron Bob stopped hammering.

'Haven't seen them,' he said.

'Have you seen a small girl?'

'What does she look like?'

'Tall as a small pony, wearing a cowgirl outfit – blue shirt embroidered with swirls, wild hair.'

'Haven't seen her,' said Iron Bob.

'Well, let us know if you do.'

'I will, sergeant.'

Little Else heard the horses gallop away.

Iron Bob lifted up the drum.

'Those are stars on your shirt, not swirls,' he said. 'Now come over here and tell me what you see.'

He led Little Else to the forge. She looked in and saw a horseshoe glowing cherry red.

'I see a lot of good luck,' she said.

'That's right! Your good luck in coming here! Now you bring your gang to me and I'll fix those leg-irons – knock the rivets out and Bob's your uncle.'

'Thanks, Uncle Bob,' said Little Else.

Firebolt's bolthole

Dear Gran,

I have a gang! I found them building a road.
Firebolt Jim led us to his hide-out late last
night. He calls it his bolthole but it's not a hole
at all. It's a shelter high up in the hills.
It's warm and dry and comfortable and
Firebolt says you can see anyone coming from
miles away. I am waiting for the sun to rise
so I can admire the view.

Your loving grand-daughter,

Little Else

XxXxX

PS I freed some horses from the knackers.

Little Else put the postcard away with the others. The sky was pink in the east. Suddenly she saw tiny figures on the road below.

'Everybody up!' she yelled. 'The police are out looking for us.'

Dangerous Dan led them along a ridge to a place called Blindman's Bluff. When the sun

came up, Little Else found herself looking down into a green valley. She saw a farmhouse with hens and a vegetable garden and a cow. For a moment she thought of her grandmother and she felt a bit homesick.

'I'm hungry,' said Hollow-Gut Reed.

Now Little Else knew she was the leader of a gang of bushrangers but she didn't feel like robbing the farm. 'Maybe we could ask for breakfast,' she said.

'We certainly could!' said Dangerous Dan. A woman came outside and began putting up washing.

'Mum!' Dan's voice echoed down the valley.

The lady looked up and waved.

Mrs Bakehouse gave them a quick breakfast of porridge and eggs and toast and honey, then she filled their saddlebags with provisions.

'Which way are you heading?' she asked Little Else.

'West. We need to get out of the district as soon as possible.'

'Will you look after my boy?'

'I will,' Little Else promised.

Mrs Bakehouse kissed Dan goodbye then she gave Little Else a big hug. 'Be careful of that one,' she whispered in Little Else's ear as she looked towards Hollow-Gut Reed.

Hollow-Gut's hide-out

Little Else and her gang headed towards the Desolation Ranges. Soon they were far away from farms and roads. By late afternoon it had started raining.

'Good,' said Firebolt Jim. 'Let it pour. The rain will wash away our tracks.'

'We'd better find a place to camp,' said Little Else. 'We need shelter.'

'I know a place,' said Hollow-Gut. 'Follow me.'

When the track petered out amongst a pile of boulders, Hollow-Gut scrambled up a steep bank. 'Here it is,' he said, pointing to an opening in the rocks.

The cave was dark and had a musty smell. There were bones scattered around the entrance.

Outlaw snorted, 'I don't like it.'

'At least we're out of the rain,' Little Else said glumly.

'Firebolt's bolthole was better,' said Dangerous Dan. 'Can't we go back there? Or better still, let's go back to Mum's.'

'No, the police might be there by now,' said Little Else.

'How did you know about this place, Hollow-Gut?' Firebolt asked.

'Used to come here with my father,' he mumbled.

'What for?' Little Else looked around. She saw an old boot and the blackened remains of a fire.

'Used to camp here and have dinner,' Hollow-Gut said quietly.

Dinner! The thought made Little Else brighten. 'Let's see what Mrs Bakehouse put in the saddlebags.' She took out bread and cheese and tea and sugar and eggs and butter and spring onions and a frypan. Firebolt made a fire and Dangerous Dan prepared an excellent omelette.

After the meal everyone felt more cheerful. They drank tea and sang songs and talked about the Wild Roaming Life.

'We move like lightning and we never strike the same place twice,' said Lightning Jack.

'That's right!' the gang agreed.

'All for one and one for all,' said Firebolt.

'Yeah!' A cheer went up.

'Always cover your tracks,' said Dangerous Dan.

'Yes!' they yelled.

'And always scatter the bones,' said Hollow-Gut Reed.

'What do you mean?' asked Little Else.

'Scatter the bones and they won't come back to haunt you.'

'What bones?' asked Lightning Jack.

Hollow-Gut Reed shrugged and went quiet. 'Just something my father used to say,' he muttered.

Little Else did not sleep well that night.
She stared into the dying light of the fire, then
she got up and stood at the mouth of the cave.

'I miss Grandma,' she sighed.

Outlaw was outside, keeping watch.
'They can't be more than a few hours behind us,'
he said. 'We'll leave at first light.'

'My socks are wet,' Little Else said.
'I don't like the Desolation Ranges.'

'We're only in the foothills,' Outlaw replied.
'Don't whinge. What sort of bushranger are you?'

'A miserable one. I don't think the Wild
Roaming Life is all it's cracked up to be.'

'Rubbish,' said Outlaw. 'It gets better when the
going gets tough.' Suddenly he pricked his ears.
'Wake the gang,' he whispered. 'There's movement
below. The police are closer than I thought.'

The Desolation Ranges

By midday, they were deep in
the Desolation Ranges.

'Are you sure you know where you're
going?' Little Else asked Hollow-Gut.
He nodded and led them into a ravine.

The track was narrow. There was a drop
on one side and a rock wall on the other.
Hollow-Gut went first. Lightning Jack,
Firebolt Jim and Dangerous Dan followed.
Little Else and Outlaw brought up the rear.

'I don't like this path,' Little Else said quietly.
'But we can't go back.'

'Yes, we're stuck between a rock and a hard
place,' Outlaw muttered as he picked his way
down the stony track.

Far below, the path levelled out and came to an end at the foot of a cliff.

'If the police come we'll be trapped,' Little Else said.

'There's a gap in the wall.' Hollow-Gut Reed looked over his shoulder. 'Trust me.'

When they reached the bottom, Little Else saw an iron gate.

'What's this?' she asked.

'A family secret,' Hollow-Gut replied. 'Come through.'

The opening was so narrow, Little Else had to take off Outlaw's saddlebags so he could fit. Hollow-Gut bolted the gate after them.

'Now even if the police found this place they couldn't get in,' he said.

And we can't get out, thought Little Else.

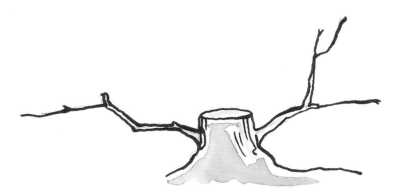

Wanted

'Still no mail from Little Else,' said the postman. 'But there's plenty of news. Look at these.'

Little Else's grandmother read the headlines.

LITTLE ELSE FREES CHAIN GANG
NOTORIOUS CRIMINALS ON THE LOOSE

'I told you you should have kept her on a tighter rein.'

'She's a strong-willed girl,' said Grandma. 'Once she gets the bit between her teeth there's no stopping her.'

The postman held up the front page of the Witt's End Gazette. 'It says here they are dangerous criminals.'

'You can't believe everything you read in the papers,' said Little Else's grandmother.

The postman gave her some handbills.

'Oh dear,' said Grandmother. 'I hope Little Else hasn't bitten off more than she can chew.'

Agnes Gap's Hut

No sun had ever reached the gully where Hollow-Gut Reed led them. Mist clung to the trees and the air was dank. They came to a creek. The water was the colour of strong tea and it swirled around their boots.

'Let's stop for lunch,' said Little Else. Her legs were aching and she felt a weight on her chest.

'No,' said Hollow-Gut. 'Keep going.'

Little Else didn't like being told what to do. She leaned against Outlaw.

'My feet feel heavy,' she said.

By late afternoon they reached a second creek. The water was black and deep. It rushed past with a hissing sound and a cold breeze rose from it. Little Else felt the chill and wished she was wearing more than her cowgirl outfit.

'I need a rest,' said Firebolt Jim.

'No,' said Hollow-Gut. 'We're nearly there.'

'Nearly where?'

'My mother's place.'

They crossed a third creek where the water was
a deep red colour. Little Else tried to be brave.

'What's your mother's name?'
she asked Hollow-Gut.

'Agnes,' he replied. 'Agnes Gap.'

'Do you have a dad?'

'Used to. His name was Trap-Jaw Reed.
He's not around anymore.'

'Do you have any brothers and sisters?'

'You ask a lot of questions,'
Hollow-Gut muttered.

They came to a clearing.

'There it is,' said Hollow-Gut. 'Home sweet home.'

Ahead of them was a broken-down hut and
an old stone barn. There was no garden, no cow
and no smoke was coming from the chimney.
A horseshoe was nailed to the door but it was
upside down so the luck would fall out.

Toothpick

Agnes Gap had the same lean and hungry look as her son. She was thin as a rake and her mouth turned down at the corners.

'Ma,' said Hollow-Gut, 'I've brought company for dinner.'

Agnes Gap smiled from ear to ear. Her top teeth were missing, leaving a gap large enough to drive a mail coach through. Her bottom teeth were lined up like a row of tree stumps.

'Good boy,' she said. 'I've always enjoyed bushrangers.' She looked them up and down. 'Who's the leader?'

Little Else put up her hand. She wished she hadn't let Hollow-Gut bring them here.

'Ah, the little nibblet,' said Agnes. 'Welcome. Let me introduce you to the family.'

She pointed to a poster on the wall.
'Meet my husband, Trap-Jaw Reed.
Look at the bite
on him.'

The man had
a nasty grin.

'And this is
Toothpick,' she said,
hauling a small boy
out from behind the
stove. 'He's the last
of my nine children.'

'What happened
to the others?'
asked Little Else.

'That's family business!' Agnes snapped.

Little Else looked around. There was nothing
in the kitchen except a chopping block,
a stew pot and an enormous wooden mallet.

'Well, thank you for inviting us to dinner,'
she said. 'But we've got our own food and
we'll eat outside.'

'Suit yourself,' said Agnes.
'You can sleep in the barn.'

Toothpick was a sorry little boy. He was pale as death and so thin you could almost see through him. He followed them outside.

'Doesn't your mother feed you?' Little Else asked.

'Not often,' he whispered.

Little Else opened the saddlebag and shared her food. Then, because he still looked forlorn, she did a couple of handsprings to cheer him up. She also wanted to cheer herself up. Toothpick smiled.

'Can you teach me?' he asked shyly.

'Of course. It's easy if you practise.'

Little Else helped him keep his balance in a handstand. 'There! You're a natural,' she said. Toothpick's face lit up. 'Haven't you ever had any fun before?' Little Else asked. He shook his head.

Little Else turned to Outlaw. 'Poor little mite,' she whispered.

'Toothpick! Where are you?' Agnes yelled.

'I have to go,' said Toothpick. Then he lowered his eyes. 'Listen,' he whispered. 'There's something I have to tell you…'

'Toothpick, get here!'

The boy hurried away.

Strife

L̲ate that night, Little Else and Outlaw stood in the shadow of trees a short distance from the hut. Moonlight poured through the open door of the barn. The gang was asleep.

'I used to sleep with one eye open,' said Little Else. 'But now I can't sleep at all.'

'Same here,' the big horse agreed.

Agnes was snoring in the hut. Little Else could hear the wind whistling through her teeth. Suddenly something moved in the doorway.

'Now we're in strife,' Outlaw whispered.

They stood perfectly still and watched as Hollow-Gut Reed slipped over to the barn. He bolted and padlocked the door, then disappeared back inside the hut. They could hear him moving about. Agnes stopped snoring and a candle was lit.

Little Else crept closer and peered through a crack. Hollow-Gut had shaved off his beard and he was wearing a fancy shirt and shiny new boots. Agnes was cutting his hair and blackening it with charcoal.

'It's a waste,' she hissed. 'Three grown men, the horse and the kid would keep us going for ages.'

'But think of the money,' Hollow-Gut replied. 'Four bushrangers and a reward for each of them. We could book into the Grand Hotel and eat our hearts out.'

'I might turn you in as well. Make it five.'

'Just try it,' said Hollow-Gut.

Agnes parted Hollow-Gut's hair down the middle and slicked it into place with mutton fat. 'There,' she said. 'Now no one will recognise you. Saddle up that horse and get going.'

'No. The horse is a rogue. I'll go on foot. Go back to sleep, Ma. I'll find the police and bring them back by morning.'

Little Else watched him leave.

After some time, Toothpick crept outside to the barn.

'Little Else,' he called.

'I'm here. I heard everything. Is there any way out of this gully except by the narrow gate?'

Toothpick shook his head. 'My father made that gap in the wall,' he said. 'He put up the gate and there's no other way.'

'How long since you've seen your father?' Little Else asked.

'Three years. He went out one day with Hollow-Gut and never came back.'

'Tell me something about him. Anything you like.' Little Else was thinking fast.

'He used to whistle,' Toothpick said.

'He whistled a special tune for Mum.
They used to whistle it together before
she lost her front teeth.'

'What happened to those teeth?'

'She broke them on my brother,
Rot-Gut Reed.' Toothpick said sadly.
'We're a tough family.'

'Can you remember how the tune goes?'

Toothpick leaned close and hummed
it in her ear.

'It's a haunting melody,' said Little Else.
She hummed it back.
'Is that right?'

'Yes,' he said.
'You've got it.'

'Go back
behind the stove.
I've got a plan.
It might not
work but
I have to try.'

Trap-Jaw

Little Else turned to Outlaw. 'I need to get up on the roof of the hut,' she said. The roof was steep and there was no ladder. 'I'm going to try the triple-backward catapult flip.'

Outlaw gave a long low whistle. 'Do you think you can make it?'

'With your help,' she said.

Outlaw got as far away from the hut as he could, then he thundered towards it at full gallop.

At the last minute, he stopped dead. Little Else was flung into the air. She did three perfect backward somersaults and landed lightly on the roof without making a sound. She put one finger on the stovepipe to balance herself.

Agnes looked out the door. 'Damn fool of a rogue horse,' she said, then she went back to bed.

Little Else took a deep breath and blew
across the stovepipe. It made an eerie sound.

'Agnes Gap,' she called. Her voice was low
and steady. It echoed into the hut.
'It's your late husband, Trap-Jaw Reed.'

Agnes Gap sat bolt upright. 'You're late
all right,' she snapped. 'I've been waiting
for three years. Where have you been?'

'In Hollow-Gut's cave.'

Little Else heard Agnes stomp
to the door and open it.

'Trap-Jaw, where are you? Show yourself.'

'I can't,' said Little Else.
'I've got no flesh on my bones.'

'Trap-Jaw... your voice is different
than I remember it...'

'That's because I'm dead, Agnes,'
said Little Else sadly. 'You're talking to a ghost.'
She blew over the stovepipe again then she
whistled the tune.

Agnes Gap gasped.
Her hair stood on end. Little Else
saw it rise over the edge of the roof.

'Trap-Jaw… that tune… it reminds me of the
old days when we were young and happy and we
used to eat sheep.' Agnes staggered back inside.
She began to wail.

Little Else pulled a couple of shingles off
the roof and clicked them together. The sound
echoed down the stovepipe. 'Hear my bones,
Agnes. I have come to warn you. Hollow-Gut
hasn't gone for the police. He is waiting until
you are asleep then he plans to stun you with
the mallet. You'll be joining me before the
night is out.'

Agnes shrieked. 'I'll pick his bones first! I'll
chew him up and spit out the pips!' She grabbed
the mallet and burst out of the
hut. Little Else watched her
run off into the night.
She was wearing boots
and a nightgown and
she was moving with
surprising speed.

Capture

'**Q**uick,' **Little Else** said to Toothpick.
'Where's the key to the barn?'

'Hollow-Gut's got it. Let's get away.
We could hide by the gate and slip
through when he comes with the police.'

'I won't leave my gang.' Little Else
put her hands in her pockets.

Suddenly she felt something.
It was the bent horseshoe nail that
had belonged to her grandfather.

'Toothpick, can you pick a lock?'

'I can try,' he said.

Toothpick's fingers were nimble
and the nail was bent in the right angle.

'What luck!' cried Little Else as the
padlock opened.

The gang was huddled by the door. Their eyes were wide and their faces were white. Dangerous Dan was trembling so much he could hardly speak.

'Little Else,' he stuttered. 'We heard a ghost.'

'Never mind that,' said Little Else. 'Let's get out of here. It's getting light and any minute Hollow-Gut could be back with the police.'

She helped Toothpick onto Outlaw and sat behind him.

'I've never ridden a horse before,' he whispered.

'Get used to it,' said Little Else. 'You're a bushranger now.'

The rest of the gang climbed on.

'Hold tight.' Outlaw took off at breakneck speed. He moved like lightning and cleared the red creek in a single leap. They were at the second creek in a flash.

'She's left the gate open!' Toothpick cried as they flew over the last creek.

Outlaw squeezed through the gate then careered up the narrow track.

'Don't look down,' he said.

Stones scattered into the deep ravine. Toothpick held his breath. Dangerous Dan moaned. Even Firebolt Jim had to close his eyes.

When they reached the top, Outlaw was in a lather of sweat. His sides were heaving and his nostrils were flared. 'This is the life!' he cried.

Suddenly they heard a shriek. 'Hollow-Gut Reed, you're dead!'

Outlaw stepped behind a tree. Little Else reached out of the saddle and swung herself up on a low bough so she could see what was happening.

Agnes Gap stood in the middle of the track facing her son. The police were behind him.

'Hollow-Gut Reed?' they said. They looked confused, but only for a moment. They jumped on Hollow-Gut and handcuffed him. 'We'll lock him up and throw the key away,' they said.

'Not good enough.' Agnes swung the mallet high over his head.

'Stand aside, madam,' the police said as they grabbed it. 'Or we'll arrest you too.'

They headed off down the steep track. Agnes followed them. 'Now I've got no one,' she wailed. 'Except Toothpick.'

Hold up

Everyone looked at Little Else.
'Which way?' they asked.

Little Else turned to Outlaw.

'What say we head towards Mt Lost,' he said.
'They'll never find us there.'

'We're going to Mt Lost,' Little Else told the
gang. 'But there's something I have to do first.'

Dear Gran,

One of my gang turned out to be a bad egg.
I'll tell you more later. I'm sitting at a sharp turn
in the road between Witt's End and Ploughman's
Bend. We plan to head towards Mt Lost.
They say once you're there you can never be
found. Apple trees grow wild and ...
Got to go, Gran.

Little Else didn't have time to sign the postcard. She could hear the coach rumbling up the road from Witt's End.

'Bail up!' she cried.

The coach driver put up his hands. He recognised Little Else at once. He had seen her picture on the Wanted poster and he knew she was the leader of a gang of notorious bushrangers.

'Please don't shoot,' he cried.

The people inside the coach stepped out with their hands in the air. The driver climbed on top of the coach and began hurling down the mail bags.

'Only one!' Little Else commanded.

She untied the top of a bag, put her postcards in it then tied it up again. Firebolt Jim threw the bag back up to the driver.

'On your way,' said Little Else. 'And make sure this mail gets delivered post haste.'

The white-faced driver returned to his seat.
The passengers got back inside the coach.

'Amazing,' one lady cried.
'We've escaped with our lives!'

'And they didn't even rob us,'
the other passengers gasped as
the coach rolled on towards
Ploughman's Bend.

'Right,' said Little Else.
'Onwards to Mt Lost!'